I0529634

MISSY'S WISH

The Lindstroms #2

Katy Paige

MISSY'S WISH
Copyright © 2019 by Katharine Gilliam Regnery

Sale of the electronic edition of this book is wholly unauthorized. Except for use in review, the reproduction or utilization of this work in whole or in part, by any means, is forbidden without written permission from the author/publisher.

Katharine Gilliam Regnery, publisher

This book is a work of fiction. Most names, characters, places, and incidents are products of the author's imagination. Any references to real people or places are used fictitiously.

All rights reserved, including the right to reproduce this book or portions thereof in any form whatsoever.

Please visit my website at **www.katyregnery.com**
Cover Designer: Marianne Nowicki
Formatting: CookieLynn Publishing Services
Second Edition: December 2019
Missy's Wish: a novella / by Katy Paige—2nd Ed.
ISBN: 978-1-944810-53-5

For Danielle, who reads it every year.
And for Danielle, who brings my PR to a whole new level.
This story belongs to you.

xoxoxo

Chapter 1

Lucas Flynn looked up as Missy Branson stormed into the kitchen of the Blue Moon Raccoon Saloon holding an empty water pitcher, her sudden appearance accompanied by a chorus of raucous laughter from the dining area, only silenced when the kitchen door swung closed.

Without stopping, she slammed the pitcher down on the metal counter under the heating lamps, then continued through the kitchen and out the back door.

The Blue Moon, located in Gardiner, Montana, marketed itself as "The Best Chow North of Yellowstone."

With the rudest customers.

It wasn't hard to put two and two together. Lucas had seen this happen several times during the four months he'd been working here.

Peeking through the order-up window, he saw three idiots in the corner, under the moose head strung with winking Christmas lights, sporting varying degrees of wet hair and clothes.

A trio of assholes.

The café's two other waitresses, Starla and Rose, hovered over them with extra napkins, while Stu, the café's owner, offered drinks on the house.

Lucas rolled his eyes.

God only knew what they'd said to her to deserve an impromptu shower. From what he'd observed, it took a lot—a ridiculous amount of mean-spirited teasing and outright abuse—to get a rise out of Missy.

Since taking the job as short-order cook at Stu's Blue Moon Raccoon Saloon after being paroled in September, Lucas had kept his head down and his opinions to himself. He wasn't interested in getting into any trouble, and he certainly wasn't aiming for any more time inside. But his lip curled as he wondered about the three guys. What had they said to upset Missy so much?

He looked over to make sure Del, the head cook, had his back turned, then glanced down at the grill where their three burgers sizzled. Bringing the spatula close to his lips, he gathered a good bit of saliva on his tongue and quietly spat on it, then he rubbed each of the burgers with a little clear goop before flipping them.

Flicking a glance toward the outside door, he wondered when Missy was coming back. It was cold and dark out and she wasn't wearing a coat. Wasn't wearing anything but that obscene joke of a waitress uniform.

Lucas had overheard her ask Stu for a larger size at least twice, and the answer he gave her was pure crap; the dirty old bastard liked the way it strained over her chest, just like all the other jerkoff patrons who treated her like dirt.

Makes me mad as hell.

He was grateful that restaurant owners like Stu participated in the prison release program, giving jobs to guys like Lucas who'd done their time and come out with a good behavior record, but Stu himself was kind of a douche. Missy Branson didn't deserve to be treated like garbage. There were plenty of people he'd met that *did* deserve it, but not her. And yeah, he got the picture. He knew her reputation wasn't lily white. Heck, from what he could gather it was probably closer to a dark gray. But Lucas Flynn didn't care if Missy had screwed half the town. It didn't change the fact that she was one of the prettiest, nicest people he'd ever met.

Lucas slid the extra-special hamburgers off the griddle and onto a trio of toasted buns. He added lettuce and tomato on the side, and three large handfuls of chips to the plates before ringing the call-bell for Rose. "Order up. Twelve."

After using the spatula to scrape the tidbits into the front bin, Lucas turned to Del. "Okay if I take my fifteen minutes now, boss?"

"Been more'n three months, Flynn. Don't gotta call me 'boss.'"

"Yes, sir." He rubbed his forehead, giving the large Native American cook a lopsided smile. "Old habits…*Del.*"

Del looked at the back door, then back at Lucas, raising one eyebrow.

"Think with your head," he cautioned, glancing at Lucas's crotch meaningfully with big, brown, world-weary eyes.

"Yes, bo—Del. Good advice."

Del shrugged, tilting his head toward the back door.

"Have at it."

Lucas grabbed Missy's jacket before slipping outside.

***

Missy Branson was sure there was a tattoo on her forehead only visible to the nastiest, rudest men who passed through Gardiner, Montana, that read in blaring, neon ink: *Available*.

Take, for instance, the guys over at table twelve tonight.

"Hey, Missy!"

It was the supercute guy who'd been a regular in her section recently. He was probably a winter hiker or a cross country skier, she thought, having noted the gear piled up behind his table. Many tourists came to Gardiner, Montana, in December to take advantage of the white winter landscape in Yellowstone—it was the best time of the year to see wildlife. Cutie and his friends had been in three times this week for supper, and he always offered her a bright smile and left her a good tip.

She stepped away from table ten, turning to face him, offering him a flirtatious smile. "Who, me?"

"Your name is Missy, right?"

"Uh-huh."

"Well…can I get your number?" he asked, leaning forward with a bright smile.

The man beside Cutie stared at the table snickering quietly, but Tess locked her blue eyes on the Cutie. Did he like her? Maybe he did, she thought, her heart thundering with hope. He always sat in her section. And he wasn't local, so he didn't know her reputation.

Maybe she'd give him her number and Cutie would

come back tomorrow night and take her out for dinner. Maybe they'd talk all night long and find out how much they had in common. He'd see what a good person she was, and—

"Earth to Missy!"

She giggled softly. "Sorry."

"So, what is it? Your number?"

"Oh! Sure," she said, taking the pencil from behind her ear

She wrote down the digits on an empty check and handed it to him.

Cutie spread it out on the table, then opened another piece of paper he'd hidden in his hand and compared the two numbers. They were identical.

"Hot damn!" said his friend, chortling.

Cutie looked up at her, a wide grin spreading across his face, and Missy took an involuntary step away from him. It was a *mean* grin. She knew it well. She'd seen it a million times before.

He pointed to the paper he'd unfolded. "Got this one off the bathroom wall. Said to call "Easy Missy" for a good time. Just wanted to be sure I got the right number."

"Slut," muttered his friend, pretending to cough.

Slut.

Missy's cheeks had burned, and her body felt tingly from a sudden burst of adrenaline. She had two choices: she could cry, or she could get mad.

Without another thought, she'd yanked the full pitcher of icy water off the tray, drew back her arm and let loose, drenching all three men and yelling "Cool off!" before bee-lining through the kitchen to the loading dock.

Goodness gracious, but men could be cruel.

What would it be like to be treated—*just for once*—like a nice girl instead of a dirty joke?

Drying her eyes with the backs of her hands, she turned when she heard the kitchen door open behind her, catching sight of Lucas Flynn before looking away.

Great. Alone in the dark with an ex-con.

She quickly chastised herself. That wasn't fair. Some men were monsters, true, but Lucas Flynn had been nothing but polite to her since starting at the Blue Moon a few months back. He didn't deserve her unkind thoughts. Lord knew how she felt when unkindness was directed at her, and it sure happened often enough.

"Heya," she murmured, making outward amends for her internal meanness.

He hung back, smelling of hamburgers and hot dogs and the warm grill inside.

"I, uh, brought your jacket," he said softly.

She furrowed her brows, turning to face him. Because of the cold, she knew the tips of her breasts would be visible against her too-small uniform. She crossed her arms over her chest protectively, reaching out with one hand for her jacket.

Instead of handing it to her, Lucas stepped closer, opening it up and encircling her shoulders, placing it gingerly around her. He tugged at the collar gently, pulling it snug around her neck and ears before stepping back.

Missy stood speechless, touched beyond words for two

simple reasons.

The first? He hadn't asked for anything in return. Not a kiss, not a touch, not a favor.

And the second? His eyes hadn't slid lower than her chin the entire time he wrapped her jacket around her. Not once. Not for an instant.

She looked at his face, not for the first time but maybe for the first time this close up. He had brown eyes, warm and dark, with a fringe of dark eyelashes. His cheekbones were high, his cheeks angular hollows. His olive-toned skin wasn't smooth and perfect, but his lips were. They were bowed and full, and Missy stared at them for a moment, biting her own bottom lip before lifting her eyes to his nose.

His poor nose.

Missy winced. Her second stepfather, a mean drunk prone to fights, had a nose like that. She was fairly certain that Lucas's nose had been broken more than once.

"Ugly," he whispered, turning away.

"N-no," she said, turning to him as he rested his elbows on the iron railing, staring out at the darkness. She wasn't a small woman, but next to him, beside his tall, lean body, Missy *felt* small, and she liked that.

"I know what I look like, Miss Branson."

Miss Branson. *Miss Branson?* If he didn't stop being so nice to her, she'd start crying again. Or she'd have to kiss him.

"Huh," she murmured, putting her arms through her jacket and zipping it up before propping her elbows on the metal bar beside his. "Haven't said a word to me in four months and now here you are, all…'Miss Branson' with me."

He stared up at the sky, running a finger back and forth across his lower lip, which pulled Missy's eyes like a magnet. Her tongue darted out and she wet her lips.

"Lots of stars here," he said.

She turned her attention to them. "I guess. Never really look at them."

"Thought you might be out here wishing on a star," he said, and she could almost feel him blush beside her as he shifted his weight awkwardly. "Stupid thing to say."

"No, it's not. It's just…I don't wish on stars."

"I thought all women did that stuff."

"Not me."

"Why not? You don't believe in wishes?"

Looking out across the Yellowstone River, she saw some twinkling Christmas lights in the distance. In shades of red and blue, orange and green, they blinked cheerfully in the darkness. Festive and hopeful, but so very far away.

"They don't come true," she murmured, turning around to lean her back against the railing and face the grimy kitchen door.

"What'd those guys say to you?"

She shrugged, pushing her blond curls out of her face. She used the rubber band on her wrist to secure them into a perky ponytail. Didn't he know who she was? Didn't he know the things people said about her? To her?

"Doesn't matter."

"Three soaked guys eating my spit in their burgers says it mattered to you."

"Spit?" Her hands froze in her hair, a surprised smile spreading across her face as he turned around to face her, his brown eyes catching hers in the dim light. "Did you spit—?"

"It was three to one. Nothing I hate more than a rigged fight." He stared at her, leaning back against the railing, arms crossed over his chest. "Oh, yeah. Except one thing. I don't like men who bully women. Ain't so fond of that either."

"What were you in jail for?" she blurted out.

Damn it, Missy! She had no right to ask him that.

"Sorry," she added, offering him a small, sheepish smile.

"I cracked open the skull of a man who was bullying a woman."

Missy held his eyes, taking a deep, shaky breath. She didn't know what to say; she just knew she couldn't look away.

"You…you did?"

"Yep." He uncrossed his arms, moving his white apron aside to put his hands in the pockets of his jeans. "Can I ask you something?"

Here we go, she thought. He's going to ask me something disgusting. He's going to kick me in the teeth with mean words that hurt more than he could ever kn—

"Will you go out to dinner with me on Monday night, Missy?" he asked.

Her mouth dropped open. "Wait. What?"

"I'm asking you out on a date."

"Why?" she murmured, feeling her brows knit in confusion.

"Because I'd like to get to know you better."

"You don't have to take me to dinner to get to know me better," she said softly, dropping his eyes.

"But that's the way I'd like to do it," he said. "What do you say?"

"Are you…for real?"

"Yes, Miss Branson, I am," he said, holding out his hand, palm up.

She looked at his hand then back up at his face. She'd kissed many men in her life. So many men, she couldn't possibly even guess at how many. But she'd never wanted to kiss a man as desperately as she wanted to kiss Lucas Flynn.

"C-Call me Missy," she whispered, placing her hand in his.

She watched him lift it to his mouth and brush his lips softly against her cold skin. It sent a deluge of shivers up her arm and down her back, making her tingle with pleasure before turning her insides hot. A small, breathy sound escaped her throat as she stared at the dark brown, wavy hair on the back of his head.

Finally, after the prettiest little eternity she'd ever known, he released her hand and turned, reaching for the kitchen door.

"Make a wish on a star before you come in," he said softly, without facing her. "It's Christmastime. Who knows? It might come true."

Then, he slipped inside, leaving her hot and alone under the starry sky.

Chapter 2

Lucas hadn't made enough money to buy a car yet, so he trudged the two miles home to the room he rented.

It was in the basement of an older couple's house, and when he'd filled out his application to rent it, he'd considered lying, assuming that no one would want a jailbird living so close. But his conscience had won out and he'd ended up telling the truth.

Surprisingly, it hadn't mattered to the Andersons. In fact, they'd lost a son to drugs, and he'd done a little time inside, like Lucas. Mrs. Anderson said Lucas had an honest face, and as long as he got his rent in on time, they were happy to give him a chance.

He was grateful to them for their kindness, and for the cookies he'd sometimes find on his doorstep, or the occasional invitation to join them for dinner. He raked the leaves off their lawn without being asked and shoveled their walkway after every snowfall. He couldn't bear to see their 80-year-old bodies doing the work that one 30-year-old man could handle twice as fast.

Arriving home, he unlocked the outside door to his basement room, wondering what the heck had gotten into him tonight: spitting on those burgers, chasing after Missy, and asking her out on a date. Though he'd noticed Missy right away, he'd done such a good job keeping his distance from her these past few months.

On his first day at the Blue Moon she'd looked him up and down and grinned, but he'd been careful to break eye contact immediately. He'd read the interest in her glance, and as much as he wanted to explore it, especially after a stretch in prison, he knew it wasn't a good idea. So, he'd kept his distance, never looking for her, never making eye contact, never being available. He needed to concentrate on holding down the job and exhibiting good sense in the workplace. Couldn't risk his re-entry by messing around with a pretty waitress.

But now? Four months later? Something had shifted. For better or for worse, getting to know Missy was more important now than it was then.

He took a cold beer out of his mini-fridge, threw the bottle cap in the little garbage can under the sink, and took a long gulp, remembering the conversation with her on the loading dock. He hadn't meant to tell her about his sister Jody and her abusive ex-boyfriend Roy, recipient of said cracked skull. He'd just wanted Missy to know that he didn't like bullies.

Lucas didn't like thinking about Jody, especially what had happened to her while he was inside. Aw, he knew if wasn't likely he'd have been able to help her, even if he'd been around. Still, it ate at him. Some days it made him almost crazy. It made him want to save someone, *anyone*, to make up for letting down his sister.

He took another a long swig of beer then ran his hands through his hair, glancing around the dingy room. The whole place was mismatched and shabby, but at least it was his. And after three years of sharing a very small cell with various roommates ranging from difficult to downright dangerous, Lucas felt grateful.

The basement apartment had come furnished with a throw rug, coffee table, and a copper-colored sofa that had seen better days. A yellow checked curtain spanned the length of the room on a long horizontal pole, cutting it in half. Behind it was Lucas's twin bed, a nightstand and a lamp.

Actually, he'd set the lamp on the floor a few days ago to make room for the miniature Christmas tree he'd found on sale at the local pharmacy. Lately, he'd been going to sleep staring at the soft multicolored lights, longing for the old-fashioned kind of Christmas they showed in the movies; the kind Lucas remembered from his very early childhood— the soft, sepia memories from when life was safe and good, before his father died, when his mother still baked Christmas cookies and told bedtime stories that ended in giggles and hugs. The kind Lucas, with his broken nose and ex-con record, knew were probably not in the cards for him.

He sat down on the sofa, flicking on the radio beside him, then kicked off his shoes and sat back.

I'm dreaming of a White Christmas, just like the ones I used to know....

Bing Crosby's voice filled the dumpy room as Lucas stared at the amber glass of the beer bottle, thinking about

Missy.

Truth told? Thinking about Missy was pretty much his favorite thing to do.

Physically, she was exactly his type: round where a woman should be round, soft and curvy with bright eyes and full lips. He liked that she wasn't too skinny; a man wanted someone he could hold on to. Her blond curls framed her pretty face, and her blue eyes were wary but somehow, not hard, like she'd been kicked around plenty, but still had some hope in her heart. Which, he thought, must make her life just about unbearable.

He'd paid special, if quiet, attention to her from his very first day, drawn to her in some visceral, unexplainable way, far deeper than his body's response to her.

He watched her secretly, careful not to draw attention to himself,

Took the garbage out when she was on the loading dock for her break,

Looked through the order-up window whenever her orders were up,

Stayed in the shadows but always made sure she got into her car safely at the end of her shift.

While on her break, she fed a mangy old dog that came around a couple times a week, cooing to it in sweet tones when she thought no one was listening. She packaged up extra food without being asked, and he'd watched several times as she threw in a few extra fries for an older couple or someone down on their luck passing through. When children came in, her pretty face would light up and she'd fish out the crayons she kept under the counter, squatting down beside them to exclaim over their finished pictures while their parents looked uncomfortable.

Mostly she ignored the meanness. It was heaped on her every other day. Women gave her cold looks while their men ogled her chest, "accidentally" bumping into her on the way to the men's room. Her breasts and ass were probably touched more regularly than the front doorknob that let people into the joint.

Why people felt like they could treat her like that, Lucas didn't know.

But he knew this: He'd treat her with care and respect.

Missy Branson wasn't garbage.

She was special. More than special.

In fact, in Lucas Flynn's tired eyes, she was rare and precious for one simple reason: her goodness was worth a hell of a lot more to him than her virtue.

And Missy Branson was full of goodness.

***

A date.

A date out to dinner.

Missy couldn't actually remember a man ever asking her out on a *proper* date, and she couldn't squelch her excitement.

The next day, Saturday, she found herself daydreaming, smiling at nothing, thinking about going out to dinner with a man who'd asked nicely, who might even treat her like a nice girl. He'd looked her in the eyes and said he wanted to get to know her better then sealed her "yes" with a tender kiss on the hand. Even if he never asked her out again, she'd have that memory. She'd know—for once—what it felt like to be asked out nicely.

The few times she'd been asked out on a date, it'd been with a suggestive smirk, so she'd known exactly what to expect: an impatient dinner, promptly followed by eager hands on her body. Pushing her panties down, they'd thrust into her without permission, but she'd let them because she craved the contact. And all the while, she'd try to look into their eyes, as they tried to avoid looking into hers.

And there were always stars, it felt like. She'd see them from a truck bed, or through a car sunroof, or from a blanket hastily placed in the dark corner of a park. There they'd be, blazing up there in the sky while she lay on her back. Always there watching, judging, cold and far away.

So she wasn't anxious to wish on Lucas's stars. They were no strangers to her, or she to them. And they both knew that a girl with the nickname "Easy Missy" probably didn't deserve for her dreams and wishes to come true.

By Sunday, however, Missy's feet had landed back on the ground and she'd stopped daydreaming. During their busy lunch-dinner shifts together, Lucas had barely glanced at her all weekend, and she started to wonder if he regretted his invitation. She wouldn't have blamed him. She was Missy Branson, after all. Things generally didn't work out for girls like Missy, no matter how much she wanted them to. She was so braced for disappointment by Sunday night, in fact, that it didn't surprise her to find him at her side as she left the café at closing.

He's going to take back his invitation. I know it.

"Can I walk you to your car?" he asked.

"I walked to work tonight," she answered as he fell into step beside her.

"Can I walk you home, then?"

She stopped in her tracks, feeling her face fall as she turned to look at him.

There was only one reason men ever offered to walk Missy home, and it was not the sort of offer they made to a "nice" girl.

All of those stupid hopeful feelings. All of that excitement. For nothing. Asking her out on a date was just to butter her up so she'd sleep with him. Of course.

Stupid, stupid, Missy!

She blinked against the sting of tears and resumed her walk.

"Oh. I'm, um, a little tired tonight. I'm not really up for—"

"Wait. Stop a second," he said, taking her gloved hand in his and forcing her to stop walking. She looked up at him, willing the tears away. She'd learned long ago that tears, like wishes, were worthless.

His smile was unexpected, all the more so because his eyes were deep and warm. Smarmy smirks and suggestive grins? She knew them well. But Lucas's smile was kind. Almost…tender.

"Hey…" he asked, "is everything okay?"

Missy gulped. "I…I'm just not up for *company* tonight…s-so I know you probably want to call off the date—"

"I don't want to call off anything."

"—because I'm not going to sleep with you tonight."

"What?" His eyes widened. "I never asked you to."

"You barely looked at me for two days! You didn't—"

His hand gripped hers tightly as he pulled her a little closer. "Missy, if I'd looked at you, I wouldn't have gotten any work done."

"You mean…you're not canceling? The date?"

"Canceling? No! And hey, I didn't mean to send the wrong message."

He seemed honest, but Missy didn't know if she should believe him or not. Nobody ever said things like this to her unless they were actively trying to get in her pants. Even then, their voices didn't ring with the truth that Lucas's did. She searched his eyes, trying to figure him out.

Suddenly, he nodded as if *he'd* just figured something out and let go of her hand.

"You know what? Let me be really clear so we're on the same page. *All* I want to do is walk you home. Nope. That's a lie. Actually, if it's okay with you, I'd like to hold your hand, too. And when we get to your house, I'm going to kiss your hand and say goodnight. Tomorrow at seven, I'll pick you up for our date." He nodded at her again. "And that's all. That's my whole agenda."

"That's all? You don't want…" She bit her bottom lip, in disbelief or relief, and felt a tear slip out of her eye to roll slowly down her cheek.

He swiped it away with a gloved finger, his expression warm and tender.

"That's all," he whispered. "I promise."

"Why are you so good to me?"

"I think you deserve someone to be good to you."

You're wrong, she thought, *and most of this town would tell you so.*

But when he offered her his hand, she couldn't stop herself. She took it, slipping her gloved hand into his.

He walked her to her door, making polite conversation about the upcoming holidays until they arrived at her house. When they got there, he stopped on the sidewalk, glancing at the simple, two-bedroom cottage she shared with her mother.

"Do you have a Christmas tree? I tell you, Christmas was one of the things I missed the most while I was inside. I *really* missed it."

Missy shrugged, not wanting to let go of his hand, not wanting to say goodnight yet, wishing she didn't have to disappoint him with her answer. "We don't really do Christmas."

"You don't *do* it? You don't like Christmas?"

She loved Christmas, but after stepfather #3 had decreed: "No Christmas crap," six years ago, there hadn't been another. He'd gotten rid of the decorations and acted like December 25th was just another wintry day. Even when he finally left, Missy and her mother hadn't really reinstated any celebration aside from attending Christmas Eve church services and exchanging a modest gift each. It was as though the joy had been taken out of the holiday and they didn't have the will or spirit to get it back.

Missy swallowed uncomfortably, hating the lump in her throat, and looking down at her boots so he wouldn't see the longing in her eyes.

Thankfully, he didn't press her for an answer. He squeezed her hand, gently flipping it over so the underside of her wrist was facing up. He rolled down her glove until the blue veins were visible, stark against her white skin, the pulse beat blinking like a beacon. Lowering his head, he kissed her heartbeat before rolling the glove back up. Then, he gently released her hand, smiled at her, and walked away.

As she readied herself for their date on Monday night, Missy hummed a Christmas carol softly, feeling excited.

He'll be here to pick me up in ten minutes.

She generally dressed provocatively for dates. Grateful to be asked at all, she was anxious to show her companion that she was up for a "good time." But, not tonight. Tonight was going to be different. Lucas treated her like a nice girl, and while she couldn't change her history, the least she could do was dress like what he wanted. What she *wished* to be.

Week before last, at the Christmas Stroll, Missy had caught sight of a girl from high school whom she'd always admired, Jenny Lindstrom, with that handsome visitor who'd been in town for a couple of days.

Jenny was all dressed up in black velvet pants, a cream blouse and a soft-looking cream sweater. The way the guy stared at Jenny, Missy understood she didn't need a low-cut dress or tight jeans that showed every curve. Jenny looked beautiful—classy, like the lady she was—and he treated her special, Missy could tell.

Thinking of Jenny had given Missy the idea to drive up to the Target in Bozeman where she could put together an outfit a little bit like that for her date with Lucas. Nothing too short or too clingy. Something ladylike. Something classy.

Missy looked in the mirror now, smoothing her hands over her cream, silk-like pants that hung loosely over her filled-out, size fourteen figure. On top she wore a new, silky, black blouse that wasn't cut too low, and over that, she wore a black cardigan sweater with tiny cream-colored dots and little pearl buttons. She'd splurged on low black heels, and on her way to the checkout she scooped up a string of pearls with matching pearl studs she'd found on a rack near the registers.

She didn't put mousse or gel in her hair to make it bigger or more styled. She brushed it back from her face and put it in a simple ponytail on the nape of her neck that curled into a sweet ball, and she tied it with a simple black ribbon. Instead of her usual heavy makeup with bright red lipstick, she asked herself how Jenny would do hers, opting for some black mascara, subtle grey eyeliner and light pink lip gloss.

Every moment as she got ready, she thought about Lucas Flynn. He had to know she had a bad reputation. And yet, he'd treated her with respect, like he wanted to get to know her despite the way she'd lived her life so far. The way he looked at her made Missy wonder about second chances, about changing her ways, about finding someone who might like her for more than her body, who might even lov—

Missy swallowed uncomfortably, remembering the stupid wish she'd made on the loading dock after Lucas left her on Friday night. She'd looked up at the sky and found the brightest star, closing her eyes and hearing the wish in her head before she had a chance to talk herself out of such silliness.

A light gasp interrupted her daydream, and she turned to find her mother behind her. Emma Branson may have been standing behind her daughter for a while, watching her in the mirror, but Missy hadn't noticed.

"Oh, Missy," her mother murmured, covering her mouth with her hands. "You look so beautiful."

Missy smiled, smoothing her pants uncertainly. "You think so?"

"Swear to God, baby girl. You look like you're goin' to church…or to a wedding!"

"I'm not, mama. Just out dinner."

"Oh." Emma's face fell, jowls wobbling against the collar of her faded floral housedress. "With a man?"

"Uh-huh. But he asked me proper," said Missy. "He's nice."

Her mother worried the Kleenex in her hands, looking nervous. "You comin' back here later, Missy?"

"I don't know," said Missy. But Jenny Lindstrom's face flashed before her eyes and she changed her answer. "No, mama. I'm not inviting him back here later. I'll be coming home alone tonight."

"Even if the date goes good?"

Missy took another look at herself in the mirror, at her

outward transformation from "Easy Missy" to a nice-looking girl.

"Especially if the date goes good," she answered, just as the doorbell rang.

Jenny Lindstrom would be proud.

Chapter 3

When Missy opened the door, Lucas felt his face break into the most unguarded smile he'd offered anyone in over four years.

Man alive, she looked pretty!

For *him*.

She'd dressed up like this for him, an ugly ex-con with nothing to offer a pretty girl. His heart started thumping like mad.

"'Night, mama," Missy called back into the house, closing the door behind her.

She struggled to put on her jacket as he watched, feeling dazed, but finally he snapped out of his trance, reaching out to give her a hand. He took the lapels, holding the jacket open so she could step into it.

The smile she gave him in return? It made his throat dry and his cold cheeks hot.

"You look beautiful," he said, offering her his arm.

"Thank you," she said as they stepped onto the sidewalk and started walking toward town.

He'd seen her in little other than her work clothes, except for once or twice when he'd seen her in jeans—too-tight jeans—when she'd come in to pick up food on her day off.

This was a different girl. This was a different *woman*.

"These are new clothes," she admitted, a sheepish twinge to her voice. "I haven't been on many, um, dates. *Real* dates. And I remembered an old friend of mine who dressed up when she…"

"What?"

"Nothing. It's silly and I'm not saying it right."

"Tell me anyway."

"I saw her recently and she's a '*nice* girl.' Her name's Jenny Lindstrom. And, um, anyway, I saw her at the Holiday Stroll last weekend. She was dressed up all special for a date and I thought, well…maybe I could do that too. I could dress like a 'nice girl,' too."

It hurt his heart to hear these words, and yet she offered them without a shred of self-pity, with nothing more than honesty and a hint of wistfulness.

"You *are* a nice girl," he insisted.

She pressed on his arm, turning to him, making him stop walking and meet her eyes. "No, Lucas. I'm not."

"I'm with you right now, and I say you are."

"Wishing it's true won't make it so."

"Sometimes wishes come true," he murmured, thinking about his life exactly four months ago today. He'd had four more days left on his sentence. Locked up. Now here he was, taking the prettiest girl in Gardiner out for dinner.

"Haven't we already had this conversation?" she asked, giving him a small smile. "I don't wish on stars, remember?"

"Yeah…except you were out there for a few minutes

after I went back inside. I wondered if you'd maybe made an exception."

A slight shrug of her shoulders made him wonder if maybe she had.

"I have an idea," he said as they started walking again. "Tell *me* what you wish instead."

"Okay…let's see…" She chuckled lightly as her hand squeezed his arm. "Well, I'd wish folks were nicer to me, I guess. I know why they're not. But I wish they'd give me a chance, you know? There's more to me than…you know…"

He covered her hand with his, encouraging her to keep going, but she stayed quiet. He asked gently, "What else?"

"What else? Oh, I don't know. Well…maybe it would be nice to have a friend. You know, a girlfriend. No, two!" She giggled, and the sound was like music to Lucas. "*Two* girlfriends. And we'd make popcorn and watch 'The Bachelor' together. And they'd come in to visit me while I was working, and I'd give them free Cokes. And I wish I had"—her voice was softer now, and Lucas strained to hear her, sensing this part was especially important—"a boyfriend. Someone who liked me. Not for the—the other stuff, but for who I am. *Really* liked me. Maybe even…"

"Maybe even what?"

"No. Nothing. That's enough." She cleared her throat. "Your turn. What do you wish for?"

He glanced over at her face as they walked across the bridge, the Yellowstone River rushing below. Stopping to loosen his arm from her hand, he reached for the railing, and she sidled up next to him, resting one elbow on the metal bar so she could look at him.

"Well," he started, "I wish I'd never gone to prison. I wish my sister Jody hadn't ended up marrying the guy who I beat up. I wish that I was still a movie theater manager in Missoula instead of a short-order cook in Gardiner. But, even if I was, I'd wish for this blond-haired, blue-eyed girl I know to be my girlfriend, because I *really* like her. Because she's the *nicest girl* I know."

He turned to find Missy's eyes bright with tears. "You have to stop crying every time I'm good to you, Missy. Because I'm only going to treat you good. And I want you to—"

She surged forward, pressing her lips to his.

It was the last thing he expected, but it only took a moment for his arms to close around her, pulling her tight against his chest, tilting his head so their lips fit better together. She whimpered as he pushed his tongue gently between her lips, the smell of her tropical lip gloss driving him wild as her gloved hands slid up his chest to rest on his cheeks. Aside from the fact that he hadn't kissed a woman in many years, he was smitten with Missy, really *into* her, and holding her in his arms felt better than he could have imagined.

But he also didn't want for her to think she needed to be physical with him just because he was taking her to dinner. It seemed like the lines between offering herself to someone out of real affection and offering herself to someone for a thousand other bad reasons were very blurred for her. And frankly, unless she really liked him, unless she *only* wanted to be with him, he'd just as soon not make out with her, not fall for her, not get his beat-up heart broken.

He skimmed his lips gently down her cheek to the soft, warm skin of her neck where he kissed her lightly before drawing back to look into her eyes.

She was worried. He could tell right away.

"Was that not okay?" she asked, brow furrowed, voice breathless.

"That was *amazing,*" he answered, holding her tighter against him. If she needed evidence that he was into her physically, for reassurance, she could have it. His body was unmistakably aroused.

He pushed against her and she looked instantly relieved by the evidence of his attraction.

"Then why did you stop?"

"Because that's not how I want to get to know you. I want to get to know who you are first."

"Why?" she asked, her face so innocent and sweet, so surprised and hopeful, he wished he could memorize it.

"Because you're worth knowing, Missy. Just for you. For what's in here." He raised one hand from the small of her back to tap lightly against the side of her head. "And here." He lowered his hand to her chest, flattening it well above her breasts where her heart was racing.

"But why me?" she whispered, mesmerized.

"Because you remind me of someone," he said, taking her hand and pulling her along so they could resume their walk once again.

***

When they arrived at the Grizzly Guzzle Grill, the greeter, Sally Jansen, gave Missy a surprised once-over before turning up her nose.

"Oh, look: it's Missy."

She inhaled sharply, hoping Sally wouldn't embarrass her in front of Lucas. "H-Hi, Sally."

"We'd like a table in the corner, please. Out of the way," said Lucas evenly.

Sally smirked at Missy before sliding her eyes back to Lucas. "You want a little privacy, huh?"

"Exactly," he confirmed with a light smile, without any hint of smarmy suggestion.

They were seated at a corner table, just as he requested, and given two menus. Missy looked around nervously. She wanted tonight to be different and she couldn't bear it if one of her "old friends" showed up to humiliate her with innuendo about the "good times" they'd had together.

Her hands sweated and she swallowed uncomfortably, sweeping the room with her eyes. It looked like luck was on her side tonight. She didn't recognize anyone except for Lars Lindstrom, who was bartending. Although they'd fooled around a time or two, they'd never slept together, and he'd always been kind to her. From the bar, he gave her a genuine grin and winked in a way that was teasing, not suggestive. Her shoulders relaxed in gratitude. Maybe it would be okay.

"So," Lucas said, folding his menu and putting it flat on the table in front of him. "Christmas is on Friday. Did you get all of your shopping done today on your day off?"

"I don't have a lot of shopping to do. It's just me and

my mama."

"No siblings? Father?"

"My father stepped out before I was born. Stepfathers one and two lasted for various Christmases but didn't end up sticking around. Stepfather three didn't like Christmas, so he canceled it."

"Canceled it?"

"Threw out our decorations and told us we weren't having it anymore."

She didn't mention that stepfather one had been the first to cop a feel of her budding breasts, and while he'd never molested her other young-lady parts, he'd found every excuse in the book for brushing against her chest.

As a ten-year-old girl she'd been incredibly frightened but unwilling to rock the boat by telling her mother. Anyway, what would she have said? *Don always seems to brush into my chest while he's serving himself mashed potatoes or helping me with my Sunday coat.*

She'd chosen to ignore it instead. After a while, it didn't mean anything. It didn't matter because Missy didn't matter.

Except, maybe it *should* have mattered and maybe it could *start* mattering. Maybe if *she* mattered to someone, things could be different. She looked up at Lucas, and her heart kicked into a gallop.

"He sounds like a jerk."

"He was," she said, then added: "They all were."

"I'm sorry," said Lucas, clenching his jaw and staring down at the table.

Missy didn't mean to make him mad or bring down the

mood. She forced herself to smile and lighten up her voice. "But…but it's okay. They're all gone now."

"I'm glad they're gone," said Lucas evenly, looking up at her. "But it's not okay."

"Hey, ya'll," said the waitress, stopping by their table. "What can I get you?"

She knew that voice.

Missy's heart sank.

Margit Johnson.

Missy had inadvertently fooled around with Margit's boyfriend Cliff in the ninth grade. It really wasn't her fault; Cliff had insisted he and Margit had broken up and Missy had believed him…until Margit walked over to her desk the following day during study hall and smacked her hard in the face and bellowed: "That's for putting your tongue in my boyfriend's mouth, tramp!"

Missy swallowed nervously, bracing herself.

"Heya, Margit."

"Heya, Missy," Margit said, looking over at Lucas then back to Missy, a mean smirk on her face. "Who's this, here?"

"Lucas," said Missy. "We work together."

"New to Gardiner?" asked Margit.

"Been here a few months," answered Lucas.

"Well, Missy's just about the most welcoming gal in town, aren't ya, Missy? *Real* friendly."

Lucas acted like she hadn't even spoken. "I'll have a beer, please. A Heineken." He looked at Missy. "What do you want to drink?"

"A Coke, please."

"A cock?" asked Margit, with wide, innocent eyes.

"She said a Coke," said Lucas quietly.

"Oh, my bad. A beer and a Coke. Back in a jiff."

Missy watched Margit pivot away and head for the bar, the lump in her throat almost choking her. She shouldn't be here. She had no business pretending to be a nice girl on a date with a nice man. Things weren't going to change. Not ever.

"Don't let it get to you," said Lucas, reaching across the table and taking her hand. "Just ignore her."

Missy looked up into his eyes, his warm, kind brown eyes, and fanned her face with her free hand, trying to be brave, willing the gathering tears not to fall.

"You can put lipstick on a pig," she whispered. "But it's still just a pig."

Anger blazed in his eyes and he squeezed her hand. Hard. Hard enough that it almost hurt. "Listen up, Missy. I don't give a crap what she just said about you, but don't you *ever* say something like that about yourself again. Not in front of me, anyway."

Her eyes widened and she tried to pull her hand away, but he held on tightly though more gently.

"Clear?" he asked.

She swallowed once, then nodded as her racing heart calmed.

"Clear," she answered.

When Margit returned with their drinks and placed them down on the table, Lucas didn't release Missy's hand or look up. Even when Missy's eyes flicked up to say thanks to

Margit, his were waiting for her when she looked back at him.

"Anything else?" asked Margit.

Lucas finally looked up, his face hard. Hard like a man who'd been in prison and knew how to protect himself and the people he cared about.

"Yeah. A better goddamned attitude or a new waitress."

And that's when, for the first time in her entire life, Missy Branson's heart exploded with love.

Staring at Lucas's badly broken nose in profile, she sighed.

This wasn't just physical desire. Or desperation for attention. Or the hope that someone would like her. Or the pathetic need to feel connected to someone. This was *love*. This was the act of her heart choosing his. It had to be, because she'd felt all the rest before, and this was new. This was different, and for just a second it made her feel breathless and beautiful.

Margit slunk away, and Lucas returned Missy's gaze, running his thumb gently back and forth against her wrist. He smiled at her, and his was, hands down, the most captivating smile she'd ever seen.

She never, ever wanted to look away.

Chapter 4

Lucas stared back at Missy, marveling at the transformation in her expression as he stood up for her. It made him feel like a king, like a god, like someone handsome and upstanding and worthy of goodness in his life. Despite beating a man almost to death, despite spending three years incarcerated, despite failing his little sister and having a face that would spoil milk, the look of admiration and approval in Missy Branson's big blue eyes made Lucas Flynn feel like second chances were possible. Nothing showy or complicated. A little happiness, like what his folks had before his Pop passed away. He had a faint, fleeting memory of his father's protective arm over his mother's shoulders as his Pop's gruff voice shared the secret to happiness: *It's a simple recipe, son: A lot of good. A lot of loving. A little hard work.*

He looked at the beautiful woman across the table from him, holding her hand gently. "No one has a right to treat you bad, Missy."

Missy flinched, dropping his eyes.

"How can you live in this town?" he asked her, feeling the wonder in his voice. "How do you stand it?"

She drew her hand back and unwrapped her straw, plopping it into her soda. "I'm a waitress. I live with my mother. I've got savings, but not much. Where am I going to go?"

"Anywhere's got to be better than this."

"Like where?"

"Kitten, I hate to tell you, but they need waitresses everywhere. Bozeman, Livingston, Great Falls. Helena. Billings, for God's sake!"

Her eyes were sparkling, and her lips tilted up tentatively. "Kitten?"

He grinned at her, feeling like a giddy teenager. "If I had a blond-haired, blue-eyed girlfriend from Gardiner, I'd definitely call her Kitten."

She giggled softly, and he swore he'd call her Kitten a hundred times a day until the end of time if she'd smile at him like that forever.

"I've never been to Billings," she confessed, cheeks blushing prettily.

"Billings is great," said Lucas. "It's only a few hours away!"

"They have skyscrapers there."

"Yes, they do."

"And an orchestra."

An orchestra. *Huh.* He hadn't expected her to say that. Her face was lit by a light inside, and her eyes were dreamy. He wanted to know more.

"What else do they have in Billings?"

"So much. Um, let's see…museums!" she said, tilting her head to the side and smiling, her face flushing further as her voice filled with warmth. "And every month there's something special going on. Like, right now? They have a Festival of Trees and, um, they have a Christmas Stroll coming up. We just had one in Gardiner, but ours is way smaller."

"What else?" he asked her.

"Oh, um, they have lots of movie theaters. You'd like that, right? And microbreweries!" she exclaimed. "More than any other city in Montana!"

He couldn't stop looking at her, loving the transformation in her face, her voice, her mood, as she talked about Billings like it was New York City. Is this how she'd be if she could get away from Gardiner? Bubbly, open and adorable?

"What else?"

She shrugged, looking down at the table, grinning like she had a secret.

"Come on. You've done your research. I know there's more! What else?"

"Well, don't laugh…"

"I'm not laughing. I'm stunned that the nice girl I took out to dinner happens to be an authority on a city she's never visited."

She chucked, then said, "They have a zoo."

Of all the answers he'd thought she might give, that one hadn't come close to making the list. "A…zoo."

"Have you ever been to one?"

"Sure. But you have Yellowstone in your backyard. What do you need with a zoo?"

She gave him a brief dressing-down with a roll of her

eyes, apparently disappointed that he didn't immediately understand the appeal and merits of a zoo. "Does Yellowstone have tigers? Red Panda bears? It does not. But Montana Zoo does. And something else besides." She took a deep breath, searching his eyes. "It has a preschool."

"A preschool," he repeated. He was lost now. But utterly fascinated.

"The Zooschool Preschool." She grinned. "Remember when you asked me before? What I wished for? Well, if I could be *anyone*, in the *entire* world, I'd teach little kids at the Zooschool Preschool in Billings. I swear I'd be happy the rest of my life."

"Is that the wish you made? On Friday night?"

"I never told you I made one."

"Call it a hunch. I'm guessing you did."

"Whether I did or didn't, it won't come true, so it doesn't matter." That soft dreamy look that Lucas had so been loving faded. "Anyway, I'm sure you need a college degree to be a preschool teacher, and I never went to college. I barely finished high school. It'd be silly to waste a wish on a dream like that."

"You make me sad, Kitten," he said softly, wishing it was within his power to help make her dreams come true.

"You make me happy, Lucas," she said, giving him a small smile.

They sat quietly, then, staring deeply into one another's eyes, so taken with one another that when Margit returned to take their orders, they barely noticed how greatly her attitude had improved.

***

Missy kept her gloves off on the walk home because she wanted to feel the skin of her palm pressed up against the skin of Lucas's. They walked slowly and she hoped it was because he'd had as good a time as she—that he liked her even half as much as she liked him.

"Can I ask you something?" she asked.

"Sure."

"Two things, actually."

"Okay, two things."

"First, what happened with your sister? And second, who do I remind you of?"

He sighed, adjusting then readjusting his fingers to lace them through hers. "My sister is dead."

Missy gasped, stopping in her tracks, jerking as if someone had punched her in the chest. "No," she whispered disbelievingly.

He turned back toward her, staring at her in the soft glow offered by the streetlight over their heads. She saw the pain in his eyes, and it twisted her heart.

"Yes," he whispered.

Missy took his other hand in hers, holding it, waiting for him to tell her more.

"She was six years younger than me and our Pop died when she was just a baby. My Mom checked out after that, working long hours, never around, drinking too much when she was. I moved out when Jody was twelve, so she didn't really have anyone, I guess. She always dated these rough, jerky guys who were a lot older than her. She started dating

Roy when she was eighteen and I'm pretty sure he wasn't the first guy who slapped her around.

"I didn't like him, and I didn't think he was very nice to her, but he was older and had a little money. She moved into his condo, which was a lot nicer than the place she shared with my Mom. When I asked her about the bruises, Jody said she loved him and begged me to leave it alone. I shouldn't have, but I did. I stayed out of it. Biggest regret of my life.

"Anyway, she showed up at my job one night about four years ago. Guy from the ticket booth came and got me. Her lip was split, her nose was broken, and she could barely move her arm because her collar bone was busted. I'd never seen anything like the raw meat that was my sister's face. I lost it. I went ballistic. I went over to their place and I beat Roy within an inch of his life. Jody was actually the one who ended up calling the cops on me." He looked down. "I ended up in the state pen for aggravated assault. While I was in there, she married him. It's sad but typical. Most women return to their abuser. It's a vicious cycle."

Missy swallowed painfully. Lucas raised his eyes and they slammed into hers. His were so full of sorrow, so full of regret, she winced, bracing herself for whatever he was going to say next.

"He beat her to death one night," Lucas said, "while I was in prison."

"Oh, God. Oh, no, Lucas…"

"I shouldn't be with you," he said suddenly, dropping her hand to crack his knuckles as he scuffed his shoe on the sidewalk. "I couldn't even save my sister. I'm an ex-con. I've got next to nothing, Missy. A crappy room and a crappy job. I'm ugly as sin. I'm—"

"Stop!" She raised her hands to his cheeks and held them there until he looked at her. "You're wonderful," she said in a clear, soft voice, stepping forward until her chest pressed up against his, wanting so badly to comfort him. "You hurt someone who was hurting her. You tried to save her. You did your time. You're getting back on your feet. You'll make something of yourself, Lucas. I know it. You're not bad, you're good. I believe in you...and—and from where I'm standing...you're *beautiful.*"

He shuddered; actually *shuddered* against her, as she finished speaking. His arms came around her and his lips found hers in the dim light, more urgent than last time, fierce and possessive. He held her tightly, finally drawing back to rest his forehead on hers as a light falling snow dotted his dark hair.

"I'm going to make something of myself, Missy," he promised, pulling back so she could see his face. "I'm not staying here forever, working as a short-order cook. No, ma'am. I'm going to make something of myself."

Missy nodded once, leaning forward to kiss him before laying her cheek on his shoulder. But the sudden agony in her heart took her breath away.

I'm not staying here forever.

She was incredibly stupid to not have realized it sooner, but he'd be leaving Gardiner as soon as he got back on his feet. He'd leave her and go somewhere amazing like Helena or Billings, and she'd be left behind as she always was.

Because that's what men did: took what they wanted from her and moved on.

Missy could feel the heat of his body rising from his shoulder, warming her cheek, and she clenched her jaw. She was used to taking what she was offered and making do. She was used to taking scraps of kindness, feeling grateful, even if she had to pay for them with her body. She was used to being used, feeling sad and disappointed.

But she wasn't used to anger. It surprised her to feel it bubble up inside. She wished she'd never met Lucas Flynn. She wished he'd never spoken to her at all, never showed her something beautiful, something different. The others had been clear. They'd let her know their designs from the start. But, Lucas had been sweet and polite. He'd gotten to know her a little. They'd made the emotional connection she'd craved all her life and it still wasn't enough. *I'm not staying here forever.* He was already planning to leave.

At least you had this, Missy. At least you had this. You can live on this forever.

"You're the sweetest girl I've ever known," Lucas breathed, clasping her tightly against him.

At least you had this.

Desperately, Missy tried to believe it would be enough, wanting it to be enough, wincing that it wasn't.

She closed her eyes against the burn of tears and let him walk her the rest of the way home. Like a gentleman, he did not suggest any more than she gave, did not ask to come in—just kissed her cheek sweetly and said he'd see her at work.

Later, alone in her bed, the tears flowed freely as Missy berated herself as an idiot for not seeing the big picture sooner. Lucas was broken and sad, as so many of the others had been, but he wouldn't be that way forever. He was just like the boys she'd tried to befriend all her life, like all of the other faceless men who'd needed something from her only to leave her used and discarded.

No, that wasn't true. It wasn't *just* the same. While she'd had some modest hopes about connecting with the others, she'd never let herself fall for them. She'd given those boys and men her body.

She'd given Lucas her heart.

Chapter 5

The following evening, as Lucas flipped burgers, he couldn't stop thinking about Missy.

She'd gotten real quiet after he told her about Jody, and even though she'd let him kiss her goodnight, she'd hurried inside without another word., which confused him because they'd had such a great evening together. At least, *he* had.

Being with Missy felt better than anything he'd ever known, and he'd sort of hoped she felt the same. She made him feel like he wanted to be a better man. She made him feel like he could make something of himself despite his past. She made him feel like redemption was possible, like by loving Missy, and taking care of her, he could somehow make up for not saving Jody.

Whoa! Whoa. What?

He stared at the burgers in front of him until they started to smoke then flipped them onto buns and hit the bell at the order-up window.

Loving Missy. Love. Did he love her?

He looked through the order-up window to see her wiping down a table distractedly. She was wearing the black and white sweater from last night buttoned up over her uniform. Stu had asked her twice to take it off, but she'd refused, saying she was cold and planned to feel cold until he got her a new dress in her size. That made Lucas smile. When she was angry, she always showed a little extra spirit, just as she had with those assholes and the pitcher of water last week.

But was she only angry about the uniform or was there something else? He had an uncomfortable feeling that something more was wrong and it had to do with him. She'd rushed their goodbye last night and barely looked at him since arriving for work.

Just then, she walked through the kitchen, heading for the loading dock. She had her jacket and gloves on and was going on her break, but she didn't even glance over at him as she sailed past.

Shoot. What's going on?

"Supper break, boss, er, uh, Del?"

"Is this gonna be a problem for you?" Del asked, flicking his chin toward the back door.

"No. We're just—"

"Keep your personal business personal," advised Del. "You got fifteen minutes, son."

Lucas threw his apron off over his head and hurried to the back door. When he stepped outside, there she was, hands on the iron railing, looking up at the sky.

"Wishing on another star, Kitten?" he asked softly.

"No point," she answered, glancing at him, then quickly away.

So we're back to this. He stood next to her, putting his hand directly next to hers so their pinkie fingers brushed.

She moved away, crossing her arms over her chest.

"Did I do something wrong?" he asked.

"You never told me who I remind you of," she evaded.

"My sister."

"Your sister," she said in a soft, defeated voice.

Lucas took a deep breath and turned to face her. He'd just said she reminded him of his dead sister. He was going to need to explain that answer, and he owed her the truth.

"The people in this town treat you like garbage, Missy. And man, I hate that so much. But, by some miracle, you didn't turn hard. It's not like you're super confident, but somehow, you're still hopeful, and I like that about you so much. So, yeah. You remind me of her. Because she was still hopeful. I bet even at the end she was probably still hoping Roy'd change."

Missy lifted her gaze, staring at him with sad, glassy eyes.

"There is so much goodness in you, Missy. It's like the goodness meant for a hundred people all got delivered to *your* heart. I just want to be near you. I just want to keep it safe."

She winced and shut her eyes tight for a second before opening them up again. They were still shiny, but angry now. *Really* angry.

"Stop it!" she demanded in a half-sob. "I can't do this."

He felt like she had slapped him.

"What do you mean? *What* can't you do?"

"I can't be your bus stop or your—"

Bus stop? "What the hell are you talking about?"

"A bus stop. A place where you hang out for a while before the bus comes and you leave."

"What are you—I'm *not* waiting for a bus, Missy. I'm not leaving."

"Yes, you are. You said it last night. You said you weren't staying here forever. You're going to leave to make something of yourself." A fat tear rolled down her cheek. "You'll take what you need just like every man does, and then you'll go. It's the same. I get it! I'm the bus stop, not the destination. And then the bus will come, and you'll get on and go and you'll never look back—"

"STOP!" he yelled, his eyes burning and his nostrils flaring with sadness and pain and fury. He ran his hands through his hair then fisted them by his sides. "That is *not* true, and it's *not* fair. I'm sorry other guys dumped on you and used you and didn't stick around to figure out how damn wonderful you are, but you're *not* my bus stop, you crazy-making woman. You *are* the destination. You have to believe that."

"Why? Why do I have to believe it?"

"Because it's true, damn it. Because you're searching my eyes like they hold the key to the universe, and you can *see* it's true. I'm in this for your heart. I'll keep it safe. Don't you see that?"

"Safe! Ha! For how long? For tonight? For a week? For a month? Certainly not forever. One day you're going to get up and go. And 'safe' will be as big a joke as Missy Branson! And I'm going to get hurt, Lucas!" She sobbed softly, then lowered her voice to a whisper. "This time it's going to hurt!"

"You know what sucks, Missy? People have treated you like trash for so long, you believe it. You buy it. You don't think you deserve someone who treats you decent, who sees your goodness, who loves you, who wants—"

Her quick intake of breath and wide, shocked eyes made him stop speaking. *What?* And then it occurred to him. He was *yelling* at her. For a while now. An ugly ex-con who once beat someone's brains in was *yelling* at her. Probably scaring her to death. Scaring Missy. *His* Missy.

"Hey…" He took a deep breath. "I—I'm sorry I yelled at you." Mouth still ajar, she stared back at him, saying nothing, so he continued on. "But you know what, Missy? If you can't trust me, if you can't even *try* see yourself the way I see you…? No chance in hell this woulda worked out anyhow."

He gave her one last look of frustrated longing, but her face was frozen in shock, so he turned and walked back inside, leaving her alone just like she wanted.

***

Who loves you.

Who loves you. Who loves you. Who loves you.

Who loves…*you.*

You, Missy.

She stared at the kitchen door in a daze before turning back to the railing and clutching it in her gloved hands. He'd yelled that he loved her. She didn't care if he yelled at her every day for the rest of her life as long as those were the words he yelled.

He *loved* her?

She smiled into the darkness at the words that changed everything.

Her ridiculous wish—the wish he'd told her to make on a star last Friday night—had suddenly, unbelievably, come true. She'd clenched her eyes shut that night and before she could stop the thought from forming in her head, she'd heard the words: *I wish for someone to love me.*

He'd been right, after all.

Wishes do come true at Christmastime.

She took a deep breath of the fresh, cold mountain air, wondering how those blinking Christmas lights in the distance had gotten so much closer in a week. He *loved* her.

Her smile faded as she thought of the hurt on his beloved face.

She'd been so untrusting, so suspicious. All she wanted, all her life, was to belong to someone who would want her, love her, and when it was finally in front of her, she'd doubted it.

How could she make it up to him? How could she let him know how much she loved him too?

Christmas was the thing I missed the most…

She clapped her hands together, a smile spreading across her face as she stared at the Christmas lights brightening the darkness. She was taking the day off tomorrow whether Stu liked it or not. Heck, she'd quit and go work somewhere else if it came to that. Her first priority was to go back to the Target in Bozeman.

Missy had some serious Christmas shopping to do.

***

Lucas hated the way they'd left things on Tuesday night, hated that she hadn't come in to work on Wednesday and hated that today was Christmas Eve and she'd barely glanced at him since walking into work at eleven.

The only thing he was marginally glad about, *pathetically*, was just being near her at all. But that did little to suppress the deep ache in his heart which left him distracted and breathless and despairing.

He didn't know what else he could have done to make things right with Missy.

He'd tried to show her how he felt about her. Tried to make it clear that he didn't care about her past, that he wanted her for her heart first, not just her body. Tried to show her respect and kindness…and look where it had gotten him: broken-hearted and alone.

If he'd never known the way it felt for her to smile into his eyes, for her to touch his face, kiss his lips, tell him that she believed in him, it might have been bearable for him to anticipate Christmas Eve and Day all alone. He might have even accepted the Andersons' invitation to join them for Christmas dinner and just felt grateful to be included. But he didn't want to be with anyone but Missy, and if he couldn't be with her, he'd hole up in his dank room and wait it out. Wait out his first Christmas of freedom since beating up Roy, since his incarceration, since Jody's death. He'd read or listen to music, or heck, maybe he'd just get drunk. Whatever he did, he'd do it alone, and he'd try not to think about Missy Branson.

"Lucas."

He jumped at the sound of her voice, surprised that she was behind the warming counter and so close to him. Waitresses weren't supposed to be in the small work area.

"Where'd you come from?"

"I've been here all day."

She still had her cardigan on, modestly buttoned up with just a bit of her neck showing up top. She still had that black ribbon in her light blond hair too—the one she'd worn on Monday night. It made his heart ache to see it. Why couldn't she see herself the way he saw her? Why couldn't she see that she was kind and good and had her whole life in front of her? She didn't think she was someone worth having. Someone worth staying with. Leave her? Hell, he'd *never* leave her if she belonged to him. He'd build his whole life around her. But she was so convinced she was worthless she wouldn't even give them a chance.

"What's up?" he asked.

"It's Christmas Eve," she replied softly.

"So?"

"What're you doing tonight?"

"Nothing," he answered, turning back to the grill.

"Lucas," she said again.

"What?" he growled, facing her, angry with her for making him love her only to leave him all alone in it, wanting her, missing her.

She gave him a gentle smile, like his gruff tone didn't bother her a bit. "Come over at eight."

Then she turned and walked away.

Chapter 6

Missy wasn't sure he'd show up. Stu had closed the Blue Moon at three o'clock after the lunch rush, but Lucas had hurried out the back door and she'd missed him. Whether he deliberately tried to avoid her she didn't know, but she tried not to think about it. She wasn't able to ask if he was planning to come over or not. But she hoped he would. Lord, how she hoped.

The inside of her house looked like Santa's Workshop.

She'd spent two paychecks' worth of savings at Target on Wednesday buying up any and every Christmas decoration that would fit into her small car.

A fully decorated Christmas tree stood in the picture window, which was also roped with multicolored twinkle lights. The mantel over the fireplace was draped with greens, white lights and bright red, blown glass balls that caught the lights and sparkled. Every available table and countertop had a festive music box, Santa or snowman, and a small army of nutcrackers had invaded the china cabinet in the dining room.

She checked her watch: seven-fifty.

After lighting the candles on the coffee table, she pressed play on the CD and DVD players, the latter of which she'd set to mute. The sounds of Simon & Garfunkel's "The Star Carol" filled her home with gentle music, while on TV, Bing Crosby and Rosemary Clooney sang soundlessly about snow.

She checked on the small tray she'd laid out on the kitchen table: two cups, a small bottle of rum, a jar of nutmeg and a small plate of homemade Christmas cookies. She'd even put a sprig of holly beside the plate, just for a little extra cheer. The eggnog was chilling in the fridge and she could also offer him—

Ding-dong!

Missy jumped a foot, taking a deep breath, trying to calm herself.

He was here. He had come after all.

She smoothed the cream pants she'd worn on Monday night, now coupled with a new red cowl-neck angora sweater she'd bought along with the decorations. She closed her eyes and smiled in relief, opening the front door with a wide smile.

Lucas stood on the doorstep holding a wrapped gift in one hand and a poinsettia in the other. He offered her a tentative smile, as though he wasn't sure what to expect. She almost sighed aloud, she was so glad to see him, so glad that their quarrel was almost behind them.

"Merry Christmas, Lucas," she said.

"You got a tree," he realized, peeking around her. "Can I come in and see it?"

"Yes! Yes, please, come in!" She stepped aside to make room for him in the small front hallway. She was nervous.

Goodness gracious, she was so nervous.

He handed her the plant. "It's for your mom. I didn't know if she—"

"She's at church," said Missy, taking it from him. "She sings in the choir at eight, nine-thirty and midnight on Christmas Eve."

"That's a lot of church. None for you?" he asked, grinning as he unwound his scarf from his neck and handed her his jacket.

"I went at four…when the little ones go," she added, hanging up his coat and trying not to ogle him in new-looking jeans and a pressed white dress shirt. "Make yourself at home."

When she turned from the closet, he was standing next to the Christmas tree, clutching the wrapped present under his arm.

"What do you think?" she asked.

"I love it," he whispered, staring at the ornaments, reaching out gingerly here and there to touch them.

"That's good," she said, standing beside him. "Because it's yours. It's all for you."

"Missy." He turned slowly, his face pained, his eyes searching, waiting for her to say more.

It would be hard for her to say words she'd never said before. But she had to say them. She had to be sure he knew how she felt about him.

"For Christmas, I wanted to give you, well…*Christmas*." She paused a second, hoping that didn't sound stupid and then deciding it didn't matter. "Lucas, you've said a lot of beautiful things to me, but it's hard for me to believe you, to really believe that you'd want to be with someone like me...that you could possibly..." Her voice broke and she swallowed again, rubbing her hands together and forcing herself not to look away from him. "Want *me*. But I'm going to trust you. I promise you I'm going to try. And I just wanted to say..." She blinked back tears. "...for however long you stay, for as long as you're here in Gardiner, I just want to be with you. *Just* you, and, I mean, I just wondered if...if you'd let me love you."

He winced, holding her eyes. His voice was out of breath, strangled. "*Let* you?"

Missy nodded, taking a step toward him. He placed the present he was holding on the coffee table behind her and pulled her against him, leaning his head into her neck. She could feel his jaw clench and unclench.

"*Let* you!" His warm breath fanned her skin. "As though you need my permission to love me back when I love you so much it hurts." His lips grazed her throat and she closed her eyes, looping her arms around his neck. "I'd watch you pack up a little extra food for someone down on his luck, or ooh and ahh over some drawing a little kid colored for you. I've seen your patience when people were mean to you, the way you still had a kind word the next time they came by for a meal. I think I'm jealous of that old mutt you feed out back behind the loading dock now and then— the way you speak to him all sweet and scratch behind his ears like he's still worth something." He sighed softly. "I barely wasted a wish hoping for something good, even though I wanted it. So when I found it – when I found *you,* Missy – how could I keep myself from loving you?"

He drew back from her, looking into her eyes, smiling at her like she was the rarest, most precious thing in the world. Then he tilted his head and dropped his lips to hers, making her knees go weak as he held her tightly against his body. When he finally leaned back, his eyes were heavy-lidded, like he was drunk. He grinned at her, shaking his head back and forth like she was amazing to him. That's how he made her feel, too; by some miracle, Lucas Flynn made Missy Branson feel like *she* was amazing.

"Thank you for giving me Christmas, Kitten," he continued. "For giving me your heart. Especially because I know you're still worried about me leaving." He tilted his head, looking into her eyes, searching them. "I want to give you your present, too. Is that okay?"

Missy smiled and nodded, taking Lucas's hand and pulling him down next to her on the couch. He took the large square gift from the coffee table and put it on her lap. She couldn't remember the last time she'd had a Christmas present from anyone but her mother. She grinned up at him before tearing away the paper to find...a book.

No, she realized as she turned it over, not a book but an album.

She flipped it open to the cover page. Neatly printed she read: FOR MISSY, ON OUR FIRST CHRISTMAS. And on the opposite page: THE BEST THINGS ABOUT BILLINGS.

When she looked up at him, he was beaming.

"I ran out of work so I could spend a couple hours at

the library before they closed. I needed to use the computer there," he explained.

He reached over and turned the page. On the left side was a picture of the largest theater in Billings.

"That's the NOVA," he explained. "They do Broadway shows and operas there."

"I know it," she whispered. "I recognize it from pictures."

On the right side was a picture of a large glass building. "That's the—"

"The Yellowstone Art Museum," Missy finished, running her fingers over the pictures he'd printed of the building and various works of art on display there. She looked up at him and smiled, overwhelmed and trembling, her heart beating painfully in her chest.

Lucas turned the page, and she looked down to find a collage of microbreweries on the left.

"More microbreweries in Billings than anywhere else in Montana," he teased, quoting her fun facts back to her.

On the opposite page was a photo of the Montana Zoo logo, with pictures of the animals, and beside it was a photocopy of a HELP WANTED ad. Missy leaned closer to read it. She got to the words Zooschool before looking up at him. His brown eyes were gentle, encouraging, and infinitely loving.

"I called them to see if they were hiring, and well, they don't need teachers right now. They need an aide, though, Missy. Someone who can help the little ones put on their snowsuits and use the restroom and help out the teacher. I talked to the head, uh, lady there. She was real nice. She said, uh, that they hadn't found the right person yet."

The page blurred before Missy as his words sank in.

"You could go to night school, too," he hurried to add, "if you wanted to. You know, to learn how to be a teacher. You don't have to settle for this. But you told me if you worked at the Zooschool you'd be happy for the rest of your life. That's what you told me. And I want you to be happy for the rest of your life, Missy. That's all I want."

She bit her lip, speechless, her heart bursting with love for him as he turned the last page. There was a picture of him. Of Lucas Flynn, smiling back at her.

"And one more thing," he said, as she flicked her swimming eyes up to capture his.

***

"I *do* want to leave Gardiner, that's true," Lucas admitted. "In a few weeks. A month tops. I want to move to Billings. But I won't go"—he slid off the couch, dropping to one knee beside her, his heart beating furiously with the enormity of what he was about to do—"unless you agree to come with me."

He pulled a small box out of his back pocket and opened it. Inside was a silver ring with a sparkling stone on top.

"It's just a crystal," he said, as she stared at it, covering her open mouth, tears coursing down her face. "Someday, when I can, I'll replace it with something better. I'm a hard worker. I promise I'll work hard for you, Kitten."

"Oh, Lucas!" she sobbed.

He smiled at her, pulling one of her hands away from her mouth to hold it in his own as he poured out his heart to her.

"I love you, Missy Branson. I love what's in your heart. I love what's in your head. At some point soon, I'm going to love your body, too. But it'll be because I love *you*. You. I'm not going anywhere unless you're going with me, because you're my destination. Wherever you are, I'm home."

One trembling hand still covered her mouth as she flicked her eyes from the ring back to his face. To the ring and back again. Her eyes were wide and shocked, and he swallowed uncomfortably. Maybe he hadn't been clear?

"Missy, I'm asking you to marry me. I—I know that we haven't known each other all that long, but I bet lots of folks've started out with less'n you and me've got." He searched her eyes, knowing in his heart that she was his best chance at happiness. "Way I see it, I even think – you and me? – we're *ahead* of the pack. You see the good in me and I see the good in you. And I think that's enough for a start because we'll trip over ourselves to take care of each other. We've got the good and the loving in spades, Missy."

She kept staring at him, unmoving except for the slight shaking of the hand over her lips and the tears rolling ceaselessly down her cheeks.

It was making him nervous that she hadn't responded. He bit his bottom lip, then drew her hand away from her mouth, clasping it gently, captivated by the way it looked, so right, surrounded by his. *A lot of good. A lot of loving. And a little hard work.*

"We'll build something good. We'll work at it. I promise you I'll work at it every day of my life." He stopped talking and swallowed, wishing she would answer. His voice was hushed and wishful as he asked one last time. "What do you say? Take a chance on me?"

He heard a small sound, like a sob, come from the back of her throat.

Oh, my God, could I have possibly misjudged her feelings? Could she possibly say—?

"Yes! A hundred times, yes!"

She threw her arms around him, sliding off the couch cushion and falling to her knees beside him as she pressed her lips to his.

***

Hours later in her bed, Missy snuggled against her fiancé's chest, tangling her bare legs with his.

He hadn't looked away—not for a moment—when he'd made love to her. And when he'd climaxed, he declared his love for her again in a gut-wrenching, visceral growl that had made her tighten around him, arching against him as her world exploded into intense pleasure such that she'd never known. Nothing had existed for her except Lucas and the love they bore for one another. Nothing existed but that now.

She trembled, remembering that beautiful moment, and in his sleep, Lucas pulled her closer, while grateful tears filled her eyes. She had had sex many times before tonight, but tonight was the first time anyone had ever made love to her.

Missy Branson felt like a new creation, reborn through the love of Lucas Flynn.

She held out her hand and sighed with amazement as her engagement ring caught the moonlight beaming in through her window, the crystal twinkling like a white Christmas light. There was a full moon tonight, and surrounding it, a host of stars. One of them was so bright that it could almost be the Star of Bethlehem—or the star she'd wished on last Friday night, which felt like so long ago.

Missy stared at it hard, then took a deep breath and closed her eyes.

Not even a second later she reopened them, smiling with wonder as she snuggled up against her fiancé. There'd been nothing to request.

Now that Missy Branson was finally the sort of girl who wished on stars, she had nothing left to wish for.

All of the wishes of her heart had already come true.

THE END

ALSO AVAILABLE
from Katy Regnery

a modern fairytale
(A collection)

The Vixen and the Vet
Never Let You Go
Ginger's Heart
Dark Sexy Knight
Don't Speak
Shear Heaven
Fragments of Ash

THE BLUEBERRY LANE SERIES

THE ENGLISH BROTHERS
(Blueberry Lane Books #1–7)

Breaking Up with Barrett
Falling for Fitz
Anyone but Alex
Seduced by Stratton
Wild about Weston
Kiss Me Kate
Marrying Mr. English

THE WINSLOW BROTHERS
(Blueberry Lane Books #8–11)

Bidding on Brooks
Proposing to Preston
Crazy about Cameron
Campaigning for Christopher

THE ROUSSEAUS
(Blueberry Lane Books #12–14)

Jonquils for Jax
Marry Me Mad
J.C. and the Bijoux Jolis

THE STORY SISTERS
(Blueberry Lane Books #15–17)

The Bohemian and the Businessman
The Director and Don Juan
Countdown to Midnight

THE SUMMERHAVEN SERIES

Fighting Irish
Smiling Irish
Loving Irish
Catching Irish

THE ARRANGED DUO

Arrange Me
Arrange Us

ODDS ARE GOOD SERIES

Single in Sitka
Nome-o Seeks Juliet
A Fairbanks Affair
My Valdez Valentine
Kodiak Lumberjack

STAND-ALONE BOOKS:

After We Break
(a stand-alone second-chance romance)

Frosted
(a stand-alone romance novella for mature readers)

Unloved, a love story
(a stand-alone suspenseful romance)

**Under the sweet-romance pen name
Katy Paige**

THE LINDSTROMS

Proxy Bride
Missy's Wish
Sweet Hearts
Choose Me

Virtually Mine
Unforgettable You
My Treasure—all new!
Summer's Winter—all new!

Under the paranormal pen name
K. P. Kelley

It's You, Book 1
It's You, Book 2

Under the YA pen name
Callie Henry

A Date for Hannah

ABOUT THE AUTHOR

New York Times and **USA Today** bestselling author **Katy Regnery** started her writing career by enrolling in a short story class in January 2012. One year later, she signed her first contract, and Katy's first novel was published in September 2013.

More than forty-five books and three RITA® nominations later, Katy claims authorship of the multititled Blueberry Lane series, the A Modern Fairytale collection, the Summerhaven series, the Arranged duo, and several other stand-alone romances, including the critically acclaimed mainstream fiction novel *Unloved, a love story*.

Katy's books are available in English, French, German, Hebrew, Italian, Polish, Portuguese, and Turkish.

www.ingramcontent.com/pod-product-compliance
Lightning Source LLC
Chambersburg PA
CBHW060955120626
46557CB00003B/1170